Bel Mooney   Marga: ı

Mr Tubs is LOST!

ric
of

Blue Bananas

For Sophie Rose Evans

B.M.

For Anne Veronica

M.C.

EGMONT
We bring stories to life

Book Band: Purple

First published in Great Britain 2004
by Egmont UK Ltd.
239 Kensington High Street, London W8 6SA
Text copyright © Bel Mooney 2004
Illustrations copyright © Margaret Chamberlain 2004
The author and illustrator have asserted their moral rights.

"TEDDY BEARS PICNIC" Words by Jimmy Kennedy and
Music by John W Bratton © 1932, M Witmark & Sons, USA
Reproduced by permission of B Feldman & Co Ltd, London WC2H 0QY.

Paperback ISBN 978 1 4052 0586 3
10 9
A CIP catalogue record for this title is available from the British Library.
Printed in Singapore

Mr Tubs's favourite song

If you go down to the woods today
You're sure of a big surprise.
If you go down to the woods today
You'd better go in disguise.
For every bear that ever there was
Will gather there for certain because
Today's the day the teddy bears have their picnic!

Mr Tubs liked to go everywhere with Kitty. He knew she needed him to look after her.

Mr Tubs knew that Kitty was always losing her things.

But he knew where everything was.

Some days Kitty even lost Mr Tubs!

She'd race around the house yelling,

'Mr Tubs, where are you?'

All he could do was just lie there and

wait to be found.

Then Kitty would cuddle him and whisper, 'Promise you'll never run away again, Mr Tubs, cos I'd miss you sooooooo much!'

When Kitty got into trouble he tried to help her. But sometimes Kitty was too busy (or cross) to hear him.

One sunny day Mum and Dad told Daniel and Kitty they were all going to the woods for a picnic. Mum was already making sandwiches.

'Can we have peanut butter?' Kitty asked. 'It's Mr Tubs's favourite.'

They all piled into the car. Mr Tubs sat on Kitty's knee. As the trees sped by he felt very cheerful.

Kitty sang Mr Tubs's favourite song at the top of her voice, and the others joined in. It was true – he did like going down to the woods.

Today's the day the teddy

bears have their picnic!

Come on, Team!

When they got to the woods, Dad gave each person a job. He took the heavy picnic backpack.

13

Mum carried the cool
bag and her basket.

Dan carried

the rug.

Kitty carried a rounders
bat and a red ball.
Mr Tubs held on to
Kitty's arm, just in
case she got lost.

It was a beautiful day. The woods looked magical. As they walked to their favourite spot Mr Tubs dreamed of real bears, waving to him from the bushes.

The birds sang, the leaves rustled, and Mr Tubs felt very happy. He sat under a tree and watched his family play rounders. 'You can keep score, Mr Tubs' Kitty called – and so he did.

At last they stopped to eat their food.

They had sandwiches, apples, crisps,

little cakes and chocolate biscuits,

with apple juice and water to drink.

Yum, honey sandwiches!

Everything was perfect, until . . .

. . . Kitty got **cross**.

'You took the last peanut butter sandwich, Dan!' she yelled. 'It's not fair!'

'Kitty's so gree–eedy,' teased her brother in a sing song voice, making her crosser than ever.

She jumped up and chased him
around the clearing, but he danced
in front of her, always out of reach,
waving the last sandwich.

Mum and Dad told them to stop but
they took no notice.

Kitty stumbled over the edge of the rug, and fell against the picnic backpack, knocking it over. Luckily she didn't hurt herself but she did kick over Mum's basket, scattering her purse, some tissues, a comb, and a bag of sweets.

Oh, no!

Very cross, Mum jumped up,
shouting, 'Oh, Kitty!'

Mum didn't notice that she'd
accidentally caught poor old
Mr Tubs with her heel and rolled
him over backwards, so he was
hidden under a bush.

Look what you've done!

'It's all Dan's fault,' wailed Kitty.

'Your fault for being greedy,' muttered Dan.

It's not Kitty's fault!

Dad sighed and said, 'Why is it that you kids spoil things? Come on, I think we should pack up and go home.'

Time to go.

Mr Tubs lay behind the leaves. He could just see his family packing up, and waited for Kitty to come and find him.

But Kitty was still hot and cross. She was unhappy too, because she knew she shouldn't have chased Dan.

She wanted to say 'I'm sorry' to Mum, but the words got stuck.

It didn't take long to pack up. Soon they were ready to leave. All Kitty could think about was how bad she felt. The others were sad the day was spoiled. Nobody remembered Mr Tubs. They began to walk back to the car.

Mr Tubs heard their soft footsteps getting fainter and fainter.

Coo!

Then suddenly all he could hear was the song of the birds.
An ant ran over his nose.
Mr Tubs felt very alone.

Tweet!

27

He lay there, waiting for Kitty to

come running back through the trees.

He knew she couldn't go to sleep

without him, and felt very worried.

A fly landed on his ear.

Mr Tubs thought he heard it buzzing,

'Nobody wantzzzz you,

Mr Tubszzzzzz.'

Many hours passed.

The afternoon got smaller
and smaller as the evening
came, and Mr Tubs's little
furry heart got smaller and
smaller too.

Help!

Suddenly the sun wasn't there any more. The shadows grew long.

Mr Tubs thought about Kitty, as if wishing would make her come back. But she didn't.

Kitty will be having her tea now.

It was darker now. Mr Tubs
saw the first star through the
leaves. Then he heard a
rustling and felt afraid.

31

But when he saw the little rabbit

twitching its nose, he smiled. Bears

aren't afraid of rabbits,

after all.

I'm not scared
of the dark,
either.

Time passed. There was a snuffling

sound quite near his head. What

could it be? Mr Tubs wanted to shout

'Go away!' but he couldn't.

When he saw the sharp eyes of the fox he was very scared. But the fox knew a teddy bear wouldn't be good to eat and went on his way. He was looking for the rabbit . . .

Yuck! Who wants to eat a toy?

The next animal to come along was a
small deer. She peered under the bush
with her soft brown eyes. Her breath
was warm.

Mr Tubs was sure

he heard her whisper, 'Are you lost,

little bear?' She seemed so gentle he

wished he could go with her.

In the tree above, the owl cried,

'Whoooo . . . loooost . . . yoooooou?'

Are you lost?

Kitty loves me really!

Suddenly the deer danced away.

Something had frightened her.

To Mr Tubs's horror, a snake slithered up to his head. Her eyes glittered like little black buttons.

'Ssssssilly sssssssoft Tubsssssss,' she hissed, but didn't stop long enough to let him growl.

He would have frightened her right back,

that's for sure.

Kitty always said she didn't like snakes,

and he knew he had to look after her.

Don't you scare my Kitty!

Sssssssssss!

Oh . . . but he forgot. Kitty wasn't there.

Mr Tubs felt something tickle his ear.

A tiny vole had crept up to him and snuggled by his head to keep warm. This was such a nice feeling it reminded Mr Tubs of being in bed with Kitty. That made him very sad.

Go to sleep, little vole.

Suddenly two sets of eyes gleamed in the darkness. Mr Tubs felt the little vole shiver. Knowing he had to look after him, he glared back at the scary eyes and sent his biggest, deepest growl rumbling through the gloom.

GRRRRR!

The two stoats yipped in terror and scampered away.

Oh, thank you,
Mr Tubs!

Now Mr Tubs felt very
brave. I may be little, but I'm
being a real bear, he thought. He knew
that if there were any big bears in that
wood (and who knows? There might
be . . .) they'd take him with them as
one of the gang.

Time to go
home, Mr Tubsy.

Suddenly there was a rumble and a crash. Something big was coming. Mr Tubs thought about those real bears and gulped. What if they didn't like little bears who smelt of human cuddles? But the animal looking at him now had a big snout and a black and white face.

The little vole ran away with a tiny squeak.

Help!

It was a badger!

But the badger didn't stay long. He
lumbered away at the sudden sound
of footsteps. The bright beam of a
torch made a path through the
darkness of the woods.

Mr Tubs heard a voice

say, 'Where were we today?

I think it was here . . .'

Then his heart went

pitter-patter.

. . . and there was Mr Tubs.

Dad swept him up with

a whoop of joy.

Back home, Dad

crept into the house

and up the stairs.

Kitty was in bed.

She had been crying. Dan and Mum were trying to comfort her. 'I want Mr Tubs,' sniffed Kitty. 'He'll be cold out there.'

'Don't worry, pet, I know Dad will find your bear,' said Mum.

Mr Tubs!

'Of course he will,' said Daniel.

Just then Dad ran into the room,

waving Mr Tubs in the air.

Kitty snuggled down with her bear.

'But you promised me you'd be good

and not run away,' she whispered.

Mr Tubs wanted to tell her she'd got it

wrong. It was Kitty who had lost him!

But he knew he'd just have to look

after her a bit better from now on.